SALLY
A SOLO PLAY

BY SANDRA SEATON

East End Press

SALLY
© Copyright January 2003 by Sandra Seaton

March 2018 Edition

ISBN: 978-0-9968152-3-9

Printed in the United States of America

ACT ONE

Note to actor: Unless otherwise identified, the speaker is Sally Hemings in March, 1826. All other voices are identified in parentheses before their lines.

The Mister, Thomas Jefferson, hasn't been well lately.

His daughter Patsy, her eleven children and various cousins and nephews. Roaming about…

(calls out in the direction of Patsy) I'll be right there.

(to herself) Patsy's calling me again. Trying to pretend as if all this is nothing out of the ordinary. Just another day. Nothing to talk about but the menu for dinner. Enough of that.

I'm sure you can see this isn't a good time to raise a fuss, what with the Mister ill and everyone so concerned, but years ago he promised my children their freedom, and I returned to Monticello 38 years ago because of it. I think I made the right decision back then. And if I didn't, I'll know by the end of the day.

I've lived in this house as long as I can remember. When my sister Martha married Thomas Jefferson, I was three years old **(holds up three fingers)**. In 1776, I arrived here as a part of her inheritance. One other thing: her father John Wayles had three wives. After his third wife died, my mother Elizabeth Hemings became the common-law wife of John Wayles, bore him five children. That made me half-sister to Mistress Martha.

I was in that room over there when my half-sister Martha Wayles Jefferson passed on. She called me to her side and asked for my hand.

1

(as Martha Jefferson) Here, Sally, keep this bell.

The bell she rang when she needed me. We never knew what ailed her. I was nine years old.

The way of putting my hands like so, I get those ways from her.

They say I was born old, so so old before my time. I stood by mother, under the canopy bed, saw Mistress Jefferson raise four fingers. Why, I'll never know. Heard Mother's voice: Sally, pray for your dear sister. The master, tall, straight back bent in grief, swore he'd never wed again.

My mother, Elizabeth Hemings, called him "a giant of a man." Oh, how I miss her. Master Jefferson took to his bed. For days, he couldn't be roused. Never saw a man in so much pain. When Burwell brought meals to his chambers, **(points off the stage)** his "sanctum sanctorum" he called it, they say he barely raised his head. Didn't want to see a soul. The fevers that gripped him. We thought he'd never come back to us.

(as young Sally) Mother, may I take the pot of tea to the Master? Mother?

(as her mother) You? go running off with the Sevrés?

(as young Sally) But I'll be careful.

(as her mother) Sally Hemings, great breaker of china, don't you know by now?

(as young Sally) But mother…

(as her mother) No one's allowed in his rooms. No one except Burwell.

2

As soon as my mother's back was turned, I would ease up to the door and quick, try to peer into the room. Blocked again by a stack of books.

(Walks to another part of stage)

Who's that peering around out there? **(Looks out window)** Never seen that face before. Probably another creditor.

Let's see if I can get some more sunlight in here. That wall over there, they're planning to tear it down soon.

When Monticello was new as a babe, I played the whole day. Back then, I spent most days with Mistress Jefferson's daughters, my niece. Martha. I was their companion. Let me explain—about the two Marthas. My sister, Martha Wayles Jefferson, the Master's first wife, gave painful birth to a daughter, her namesake, Martha. We all call her Patsy. You see, Patsy and I are the same age. Oh, I know it's confusing.

There were two families, the official family—John Wayles, his daughter Martha and his other children by his first wife, and the unofficial family—my mother Elizabeth Hemings and her five children with John Wayles—me, Sally, James and three more.

We played over there—by that poplar tree. Climbed the shrubs under his window, but the master had locked himself away, too far away to hear our shouts and screams.

(as Patsy) Hurry, Sally. Don't let the boys catch us.

(as young Sally) I won't. **(screams)** first one to reach the tree is a blind beggar. This way, Patsy. Down the hill. Hah. Fooled you. Missed it by a mile.

Hands clasped together, in the shade of his poplar tree, we skipped and stopped, spied his words on her grave: *If in the House of Hades, men forget their dead, yet will I remember my dear companion.*

When we weren't playing hide-and-go-seek by his window, I was devising schemes to hide Patsy's books under my bed.

(as young Sally) Here Patsy, let me hold the book. We'll pretend. Stuff your gown with these old rags, take best dolly in your arms. Put sweet girl to the breast. Like so. **(to the audience)** If I break another dish, I won't have to wash the Sevrés again!

That was over forty years ago. **(She looks off to the side.)** I never thought I'd see him ill again—never the way he is now. These days there's a constant parade of people in and out of his private rooms. His sanctum sanctorum.

Is that broth you're taking into him? **(to Burwell)**

There'll be those who won't want me to go into see him, but I'll go in anyway.

Patsy's been trying to get my attention all day. I can tell something's going on with her. Usually she doesn't wait, she ups and says whatever she's thinking. It's her way. Her birthright.

(to Patsy) Mistress Randolph.

Patsy's married to Thomas Mann Randolph, that Randolph man, he's not the easiest one to get along with.

(to Patsy) Mistress Randolph, is there something I can do?

4

When I call her Mistress Randolph, she gives me the funniest looks. Thinks I'm being clever. What else would I call her? There she is in the hall. **(Walks to her)**

(as Patsy) Sally, I don't know how I'll be able to keep up with everything.

Her fingers are swollen and bent as if she's been out in the cold too much, but I think it's from all the worrying. Patsy worries all the time. About her children, about another scandal, everything. What with the Mister so deep in debt…

The Mister. When I was a girl, after we came back from France—when we were alone, of course—I began to call him "Mister," as is the custom with married folks. He never corrected me.

(Goes to the side of the stage) Tonight I'll leave this light on so Patsy can see. Every evening she takes longer and longer to make her way up the stairs.

My mother Betty Hemings worried about her children too. You can't quite see this, but if you look over there, see that road? That's where an overseer from the next farm chased down three brothers and beat one so badly that he bled to death right there on the road.

She tried to keep me near her, but the boys around Mulberry Row (that's what we called our folks' cabins) those boys, young Jack and Mary's John, they followed me everywhere. Summer evenings, mother made me stay inside.

(young Sally) Now, mother. Mother, I'm not a child…
Young Jack's son and Mary's boy? It was only for help with

their crop. Young Jack says he's seen no hair like mine. Beauty itself.

My mother Elizabeth Hemings grabbed me by the collar and marched me inside.

In 1784, the Master accepted a post overseas, Ambassador to France. All the grief from the death of the Mistress—her memory was driving him away.

You might have heard this before—the Mister was known for the most lavish entertaining. Nothing too costly or too rare to bring to his table. Of course, he was no different from the other planters. Thirty-two covered dishes for a guest or two. He thought nothing of it. That's why my brother James had to go along, to be trained as a French chef.

(as her mother*)* Sally, a letter came today from your brother James.

I reach for the letter but Mother holds it away from me.

(as her mother*)* He is well. Some days he goes to the kitchen at the Hotel Langeac before dawn, as early as four in the morning and he does not leave till after dusk. The work is brutal, and he wonders if it is possible to ever learn to cook all the French dishes, but he says the nights are warm and lovely…

"Warm and lovely" … I pounce on those words. James must be out and about, gathering flowers for handsome women, sitting by the lake till dawn. I want to know about James's nights. I strain to read the words, only to have them snatched away. Mother folds the letter and places it firmly in her lap.

(as her mother) Master Jefferson says you are to accompany Patsy to France… Sally?

(as young Sally) France? I hear the words, but sometimes when words are new and strange, they're only words.

(as her mother) You will sail with Patsy to France. Here, these handkerchiefs. Keep yourself presentable. Don't wear your skirt that way. Is that mud on the hem? Cleanliness, Sally. Keep these handkerchiefs and wash them often. And child, try to act as your age requires.

I held up a beaded purse for my mother, the eye of her needle poised to make a fancy stitch. They say I favor the old Mistress, my half-sister Martha. My way of putting my hands like so.

(as young Sally) I'll go but I'll come back.

(as her mother) Sally, it's time you thought about your future.

The only one I ever knew to cross the sea was my mother's mother Beya Beyah. An innkeeper had given her to Captain John Hemings for the night to please him after he was finished with his evening meal. I can't begin to tell you all the stories my mother knew about her people—"pure-blood Africans" she called them. She would tell me the same stories over and over.

(as young Sally) Mother, please tell me again, tell me your mother's story.

(as her mother) Sally, it's time you realized… you're not a child, not any more, Sally.

She reached for my hand, **(holds her hand out)** held it so tightly… I could feel the blood drain from me. When my mother had something to say, you listened.

All those books over there. My mother helped the Mister sort those out. There's some that still need to be catalogued. My mother's gone and he probably won't get to it. Not now. My mother, Elizabeth Hemings, she had hands, stronger than any man's, I held on to her as tightly as she to me.

It seemed only days later. I was taking Patsy's hand as we walked up the plank. The captain bowed, one flourish after another, until I was dizzy with his infernal bowing and scraping and the salty, fresh smell of the sea.

…

(as captain—deep voice) Here, Miss Martha—

That was Patsy's real name—

(as captain) Here, Miss Martha… your room. And yours… **(looks down at Sally)**

Whenever the captain would stand by me longer than was necessary, I would run.

I ran nearly every day. I heard him telling one of the men "That one's crazy as a coot. Got no business caring for a little princess." He called her his princess, his little pet.

When the captain looked for Patsy, he saw me too, standing right next to her.

(as captain) "The two of you, you're awful close." When the ship's cook called "Miss Martha," I ran to the dining room too.

I could hear my mother, feel her hand taking mine. My mother's hands. Elizabeth Hemings, she had hands, strong as any man's. And when I looked into her eyes, I could see it all. She taught me how to read a face, study a smile, catch a frown—a most distinguished thing, a frown.

Later that day, when the captain knocked on our door, I pretended not to hear.

My first time on the water. White waves. If you've been at sea, all the rocking and churning, you know the way it preys on your mind.

That night I dreamt a bitter dream. Beya Beyah, my mother's mother, in the lower deck. Wet and cold in the blue black night.

A thin veil of fog. Dahomey child. **(trying to make things out)** Each dawn she climbs the palm tree and touches wine with her hands. **(still trying to make things out)** A tall boy. A farmer's son. Her family leads him down the road. Marriage. The gods must have a hand in this! A young goat sacrificed, okra, oranges, a basket of yams laid at her feet. She stands with old friends, her buba and iro an odd-colored blue, hair in beads, piled to the sky, tapping the palm wine from the palm tree.

Kidnapped. Before the roast meat was cold, snatched away to America; she was a stranger to the sea. White waves in the blue-black sea till we land in port.

I'd never seen sun like the sun that day. Not a bit of shade.

Master Jefferson couldn't be there, so he sent Mistress Abigail Adams to meet us at the dock. She wore a white straw bonnet with a wide-plaited crown that seemed to move mysteriously—on its own—when she peered at us.

At first she smiled, then she raised her eyebrows like so, then she produced the most enormous frown that periodically vanished and reappeared then vanished and reappeared again beneath her bonnet. **(covers her eyes)** The heat from the sun was unbearable. The bonnet seemed to move mysteriously as if under its own power. It made me worry for her safety, whether she would have the strength to make the return trip to her own home, bonnet and all.

She examined my dress, one hand to her forehead, **(pretends to examine clothing)** loath to touch the tattered collar of my waist—a near faint that changed to a loving sigh when she caressed the frayed hems of Patsy's skirts.

Mistress Abigail Adams bought clothes, for me and for Patsy. All the more presentable for the boulevards of Paris. The clothes I had washed and ironed the three months we were on board the ship were thrown away.

Paris

Have you ever felt as if you could barely hold your own? I'd never seen anyone the likes of those people—the high-born women made up in rouge, cheeks all powdered, strutting along with a ribbon dangling here and there. Why, I'd lived my whole life on a farm. Was this all a dream?

We lived on the western edge of Paris at the intersection of the Champs Elysees and the Rue de Berri at the Hotel Langeac, a perfect view of the annual Promenade Longchamp**, (marches, then struts)** where all the rich folks, the aristocracy of Paris, and even the poorest workers parade in their finest.

Patsy and I stay with Master Jefferson. My brother James lives downstairs in a room near the kitchen. **(folds hands)**

Master Jefferson speaks with his hands folded. He is willing to call the hotel an elegant place.

My brother James tells me:

(as James) "Sally, your laugh. You are more our sister Martha Wayles than she was herself."

Our rooms in Paris were spacious. Here at Monticello, Patsy and her husband live upstairs in those cramped quarters. Eleven children in those tiny rooms. How does she ever sleep at night with so little room? Sometimes I accuse her of stinginess, but what does the poor woman have to give when she has so little for herself? I spend part of my time in the Mister's chambers, the rest in a little room underneath a wing of the house.

Even now, when he's not so well, Mister still wants things just so. Never mind how *he* looks—in his old brown coat and socks that don't match. Never mind that. A woman must dress properly. Not a wrinkle, nor a speck of dirt.

There goes Eston running by with his fiddle tucked under his arm. Eston **(tries to catch up with him but fails)** Our son Eston brings music to the sitting room, a fine fiddle to soothe the Mister's head.

I remember the first time he noticed me. I mean noticed me—not the way he noticed me when I was a little girl but something—you know.

In Paris, I was rich with family.

(young Sally) Patsy? You don't remember your mother's laugh. Not at all? You don't remember her voice? Master, is it true that Patsy never heard her mother's voice or her laugh? **(walks away as if memorizing something)**

He stopped, didn't speak. Everything was so quiet. I put my hands—like this—to my hair, my dress. Was there something I needed to do? He was always so particular. Maybe my hem was torn. The master walks toward me. He surveys my brow, a lock of hair near my shoulder. He nods and walks on.

In France, I learned to style hair in the fashion of the day, to be a lady's maid, to launder fine linen and silk, embroider with all the fancy stitches I learned back home from Mother.

I am free to sample all the dishes set before me.

Saumon froid—garnished with cherry tomatoes, tarragon and those tiny little things I grew to love: **(laughs)** capers. Floating Island, and creme moulee a la vanille.

Patsy and I sneak little cloth bags filled with vanilla sugar, praline powder and cream puff paste that drips and oozes in Patsy's pocket. Ah, but the Charlotte Russe that James brings back at night from the kitchen. It was indescribably delicious. When I returned to our country, I knew things I hadn't known before.

(Walks around and looks at the floor.) There's one and another one. The Mister would raise the biggest fuss if he saw these nails over here. No one stooped to pick them up. Things are a mess around here, all the tearing up and putting back, it's still going on without him.

I complain to myself, but you know I'd like to see him again, strolling by those trees out there, examining the bark with a pad in his hands. **(Beat)**

There's a possibility he'll never be well again. He's 83 years old—not exactly a babe. He's Thomas Jefferson! A man who knows when it's time to put his affairs in order. Now it's time for me to do the same thing. I'm afraid to put it off any longer.

He's used to being in charge of everything, keeping track of this person and that one. That's why my brother went along to Paris with him.

(looking back)

James, I see you there… for a moment I thought I could make out a faint shadow.

… James was my confidant. There was never anything I couldn't talk about with him.

In Paris James worked at the Hotel de Langeac alongside free men and received the same wages they received, but, because he is James, he is easily insulted.

I'm peeking into the kitchen. My brother James is there. **(She tiptoes into the room.)** Saucissons et pates en Brioche. **(smells)** Ah, heavenly. A kitchen boy is showing him how to prepare the sheep casings for the sausage, so delicate. James does not know French. The kitchen boys are laughing. **(pretends to strain to hear)** My brother's honor is in question. James drops the casing and storms out of the room. The next morning when he returns he says his pride has been damaged. The kitchen boys speak to James as if he is their little child. James grabs a saucepan. He throws it at the wall. White sauce everywhere. He marches out of the kitchen.

The next day Master Jefferson brings him back. I watch them from the door as they enter the kitchen. Everything is quiet. The cooks stop stirring the sauce. The butcher's knife remains poised in the air. James slowly and carefully puts on his apron. Master Jefferson seems amused.

The French tutor arrives at our villa. I hurry around, dusting the room. Then I stop, pick up the book, copy the words carefully.

Excusez-moi, est-ce que j'ai trouvée la bonne place?

Est-ce que vous pouvez me montrer où est la porte?

(the professor of French) *Mademoiselle, your French? Where did you learn that?*

(young Sally) *Was this something I was not expected to know?*

He asks again, *Where did you learn that?*

(young Sally) *At the big house, where else?*

James is in the kitchen day and night, except, of course, when he is enjoying his evening stroll on the Rue de Berri. In France we are free. James insists on his rights. He is paid for his work, but I still receive nothing. I sulk and do only the necessary chores. I do them sloppily. I am warned again to handle the Sevrés with great delicacy. I hide the pieces of an apple-green cup carefully under the bed. I slow down. For two days, maybe three, I spend as much time as I can alone in my room. When I do chores, I do them slowly. When I leave to go to the market I take twice as long to return.

My brother goes to the Master. James—now he knew how to strike a bargain.

(as James) Master Jefferson: My sister wishes to be paid.

(as young Sally) In France, we are free.

Spring 1789

When Patsy turns 17, we are invited to attend social events. I am 16 years old. Master Jefferson buys me a new dress, a coat, and a hat.

James is not impressed:

(as James) Sister dear, can't you see? The Master doesn't want you to look like a slave, not here. It is important that you have a bit of status. That's right. You must not be seen as a piece of property. Not in Paris.

(as young Sally) But James— **(shows dress)** the dress is proper, not the equal of Patsy's, but lovely all the same **(twirls).** I glance at the door quickly. Master Jefferson is highly critical of women who dance excessively.

In the evenings, I dress in the new clothes. Patsy and the sons and daughters of Ambassadors from all around the world come to our apartment. We argue and argue, every time about the government in the United States, but the conversation always ends with the biggest argument of all. Patsy declares she hates slavery and all its degradations, that it is the most horrible of horrible sins.

(as French visitors) Mam'selle Sally, what is America like? Mam'selle Sally, In America, do you attend evening mass?

Here, I am Mam'selle. A letter from the Ambassador's daughter: Send my best wishes to Mam'selle Sally.

(as young Sally) Patsy? You don't remember your mother's laugh. Not at all? You don't remember her voice? She does not remember. I remember. She was my sister.

Oh, there's Patsy motioning to me again. I imagine she wants me to talk to the Mister about the creditors.

(to Patsy) I see. You want me to bring up the subject ever so gently. In an effort to please her, I make a special trip to the Mister's room. I need to talk to him myself. There's that curious fellow from the University of Virginia again. Why, the nerve! Look at him! He's sitting right at the Mister's desk.

Excuse me, sir, could I have a minute with Mr. Jefferson? Oh, thank you. Didn't mean to rush you out. **(smiles)** Early luncheon, you know.

I serve the Mister a tray of canapes on rose-pink Sevrés. He doesn't manage a smile, but his words are tender. I ask him briefly about the creditors who paid a visit early that morning. He explains to me that he has a plan whereby he will reduce much of the debt. He shows me pages filled with long columns of figures, then goes into a long lecture on the appropriate use of Sevrés.

(to Jefferson) Yes, Mister, I understand. You want the… now I understand.

We've talked about this before. I try to bring it up again— the business about his will. The mister lectures me on the domestic virtues of Virginia women, their tidy ways. The Mister is an ever-so-orderly man.

I was almost fifteen when I went to Paris. He was thirty years older, a solid responsible man with strong arms and legs, good general health, and a full set of teeth.

The Pompadour pink Sevrés had wondrous curves; a man of Master Jefferson's intellect was eager to marvel at the shapeliness of a plate.

I don't tell Master Jefferson this. I don't tell him that every day, when I look from my window, the same girl from the convent stops to meet her young man outside the house.

Today she takes off her bonnet, throws it in the air, then begins to undo her long braids. Her hair unravels in the wind, blows against her face. Are they in love? What will her parents say when she returns home?

I think I must have had quite a good figure for a young girl. I could tell by the way the men looked at me when I strolled down the boulevard with Master Jefferson. Even then he was still mourning my sister Martha.

I still tell my children about the time in France. Whenever Master Jefferson would return to the hotel, I would quickly tell him all the things I had seen from my window. Some of it was new, but other things, like the fighting, the wounded in the streets, I had seen some of that at home. I can still see the boy who ran away.

(as young Sally) Master Jefferson, yesterday, two men passed by, standing on the back of a cart, hands tied together. And today, another parade passed our window. Two men, maybe the same two, came by again. This time their heads on stakes, a bloody jacket perched behind them like a flag. Master Jefferson says the king must share power, but the king refuses.

Today a mob stormed the Bastille, slaughtered the garrison. During the next months, I could see crowds of people running past my window—fighting almost every day.

The rage, the anger, épouvantable. The sound of thunder. Tear down the gate. Throw off the chains. Another traitor sent to hell. Effrayant. The light of lightning. Storm the Bastille!

Girl, you've been here before.

I was carrying a tray when he called me.

(as Jefferson) Sally, turn this way. Now hold your face to the light. A little over.

Master Jefferson, he was whiter than a sheet. Whiter than I ever was. He cupped my face in his hands and whispered her name.

He turned to me, then I to him. It was time. Mother had warned me to let no boy unbraid my hair. Now it was time. To my eyes, he was young—a shy boy. He untied the scarf pinned to my dress. New cotton loves a hand. He said he'd seen no hair like mine—beauty itself. I felt his breath against my neck. The warmth of his hands didn't startle me. It was as if he had always held me, as if we had held each other many times before. It was time. I hear his words, but sometimes when words are new and strange, they're only words. The room was dark, but he turned away to unbutton his shirt.

Safe in his arms, but still my voice frightens him. I hear him whisper her name. Still.

La vie nocturne à Paris.

There's Patsy coming from the Mister's room.

(as Patsy) Sally, I barely slept last night. The little one was awake with the croup. The cough is all in his chest. We've done everything and it still doesn't get any better.

We hold each other and sympathize. I do love her.

(as Patsy) Sally, there's so much, so much now.

There she goes again, not saying what she really means.

(as Patsy) The will was completed yesterday. It's a good will, Sally. It doesn't free you, Madison and Eston, but the three of you will be freed just as Beverly and Harriet were.

Is she serious? There she stands with her arms folded as if she's talking about how many covered dishes to set out this evening or the number of guests staying the night. All so simple. Does she understand? Beverley and Harriet walked away from Monticello after months and months of me and the Mister planning for their safety.

(to Patsy, incredulously) As Beverley and Harriet were freed?

(as Patsy) You know I care about them just as though they were my own, and of course you, Sally—you too. But, Sally, I thought you understood there can't be anything in writing. Nothing. We've had enough of that. The scandal sheets. They're everywhere. You know what they're saying? Lies. Horrible lies. We can't put anything in writing. Not one word for those vermin to dredge up after my father's gone. I won't allow Father's reputation to be dragged through the dirt—not again. **(Beat)** Beverley and Harriet walked away. We'll do the same for Madison and Eston and for you.

"We"? What does she measn "we"?

(to Patsy) We spent months, your father and I…Making the plans for Beverley to go to Washington. Finding a place for Beverley to stay. Then sending Harriet there to meet him. Who'll take care of all that now? When the Mister's gone....

(as Patsy) When the Mister's gone? My God, are you counting the days? We've been so good to you. What do you want from us now? My poor father grows weaker by the day, and that's all you can talk about? Can't you let this family have a little peace?

She wants me to leave it alone. Give her some rest. I wish I could. Those scandal sheets. She can't put them out of her mind. Things were never the same after that. Me and the Mister. There was a time when we could plan things together. But now… Maybe I'm being selfish, bringing all that up at a time like this, with the family not knowing from one day to the next whether he'll even live. But I made my choice close to forty years ago, and now I have to see… Oh, I know there's things he never finished—but this time… this time… I have to see if a promise will be kept.

END OF ACT ONE

ACT TWO

I told you about my life in France. Why would anyone want to leave all that? The Mister insisted on returning—not in a week, not in a month. It had to be right then. **(stamps fist)** Even my brother James was frightened.

(as young Sally) James, I can't go any faster. **(runs and hides, speaks from the corner)** I'm moving as quickly as I can.

The Master is pacing the floor.

He is a god-fearing man, but he doesn't particularly care for the Catholic church, or any church, for that matter. **(moves out of his way)** He was suspicious all along when Patsy attended classes at the convent. Today Patsy has declared her intentions. She wants to become a nun. The sisters at the convent have convinced her that moral decay is everywhere, from the Palace at Versailles to the most humble cobbler's dwelling. The master is out of breath. He leans against the chair, panting and breathing. **(breathes heavily)** I try to move out of his way.

You know I wonder if Patsy wants to join the convent because she just can't stand the thought of my being with the Mister.

Servants run in and out, adjusting the drapes, removing dishes. Patsy is crying.

(as young Sally) There, Patsy...There, There.

I'm beginning to see that the Mister is really a passionate man. His skin grows redder and redder and his breathing more rapid.

(as Jefferson) Arrangements must be made. Quickly, quickly. Do you hear me? We must return.

James shrugs his shoulders. This provokes the master even more. James has found a lover, a young woman, the daughter of Pierre, the butcher, a plump girl with wild hair, blonde and wild and thick with curls. He is determined to stay in France.

(as young Sally) James, I can't leave you here. What will Mother say?

(as James) Shhhhhh… **(puts fingers to her lips as if she is James)** I'll never go back.

(as young Sally) Never?

(as James) Sally, Master Jefferson has you in a trance. Freedom, we're this close to it.

I motion James closer and closer till I can whisper in his ear. He doesn't understand so I whisper again—about me and the Master. When he finally does, he stops suddenly, then walks away in disgust.

Patsy is crying again. I grab her by the hand, and we run after James.

When Master Jefferson says we must return, that means all of us. He can't understand why I want to stay.

(as Jefferson) So you like your freedom here?

How should I answer him? Should I say yes? Should I say my freedom is everything to me?

I want to see Mother, hear her wise words. I know I don't show, but sometimes I can feel the Master lowering his eyes to my waist, then looking away.

(as Jefferson) Sally, you're a part of our family. This freedom, what would you do with it?

(to Jefferson) Do with it? Freedom's something to do something with?

No, sir. I don't mean to be disrespectful.

I understand. I do know the horrors facing young girls left alone in this era of turbulence, uncontrolled violence, death and destruction.

I do understand, sir. I'm sorry. But I can't leave, not now.

(listening) How would I protect myself? James will look after me.

(as Jefferson) James. Which James? In which one of his moods?

(as young Sally) But he will—now that he's a free man.

At first I said I'd never go back. Never. But the Master never tired of asking me. Every morning, after his bread and cheese and fruit with fresh cream, he would bring up the subject again.

(as Jefferson) If James will return for a while—just for a year or so—until I can train a new cook, I'll give him his freedom.

(as young Sally) All this to keep our family together?

(as young Sally) Here I'm Mam'selle Sally. I will never go back. Never. Morning. It's morning. The new air. The fresh bread from the kitchen. I can hold it in my hands. **(cups hands)**

Thomas Jefferson is known for being a stubborn man. He's used to having things exactly the way he wants them, and if they aren't… He offered me extraordinary privileges.

(as Jefferson) Come back to America. No work to stain your tender hands, the run of the house.

(as young Sally) My own gloves, gowns, robe à la française, skirts draped à la polonaise? Extraordinary privileges.

(as Jefferson) A servant of your own, a plate of Marseilles figs at dawn. The earth belongs to the living!

(as young Sally) At first I said no. Then he took to his sickbed. —Your head, sir, you need a fresh towel for your head? —Six long days he moaned, cried out "Come back with me." You'll gain my fidelity.

The seventh day he started all over again.

He begs me to return with him. Me, Betty's Sally. Of course I'm flattered. We would grow old together. Of course, there are things I must understand. He insists a lady should not dance after she is married. I remember the dancing in Mulberry Row after the harvest, in the evening, so dizzy I fall to the ground, but I must agree to this. In turn, he swears he will never take the floor at cotillions. Singing, playing the fiddle, the harpsichord. All these are permissible. I giggle nervously. He glares at me sternly. He pledges no other woman will share his bed. We would be as husband and wife but only to ourselves. I love him.

I go to James and tell him what the master has promised.

(as young Sally) James, I love him.

James laughs a high, painful laugh that is not really a laugh.

(as James) Love? What could you know about love?

(as young Sally) James, we will be as husband and wife.

(as James) Husband and wife? Words! You're in the fish market now. Go ahead. Strike a bargain. The children. No overseer will ever control them. No scars on their backs. They will sleep on beds with feather mattresses, **(Sally nods)** and no gruel for food. The same food as his own. **(Sally nods again)** and their clothes, their clothes will be cool in summer and warm in winter. Fine shoes for their feet. **(Sally nods excitedly.)**

(She walks to the other side of the room and begins a conversation with Jefferson.)

(as young Sally) And... **(quietly)**

Master Jefferson looks at me seriously.

(as Jefferson) Despite everything, I send you back to slavery. Your life at Monticello could never be like your life here in France—you know that.

After all his demands and declarations and promises, I was surprised when he hesitated, almost seemed to change his mind.

(as Jefferson) Patsy must never hear of this. Never.

(as young Sally) Never. But our children—I want your solemn promise: at the age of 21 our children will be free.

(as Jefferson) You have my word.

When the bargain had been struck, we packed our bags for America, set sail with three Italian poplars, two cork oaks, no apricots, one white fig, five large pears, une robe à la française.

I believed his power would protect me, so I bargained for my freedom. Not the kind I saw in France but freedom— for my children.

I learned how to strike a bargain in Paris when I was sixteen years old. Now almost forty years later, I'll do the same thing again. **(Walks across room. Patsy is at her desk.)**

(calls to Patsy) Mistress Randolph…

(to Patsy) Mistress Randolph, I have to have it in writing. Oh, I didn't mean to startle you. I said I have to have it in writing. Please understand I didn't mean to offend you. I've heard of too many cases where folks have made promises… I know, I know, you're not like that.

Glory be to God, I know President George Washington freed his slaves. But he didn't have all her father's creditors calling on him day and night.

Mistress Patsy Jefferson Randolph thinks we're finished with our conversation. She's at her writing table, busying herself with her correspondence. I'll go over quietly.

She sees me but she looks away. I can tell when she's annoyed—or maybe I've hurt her.

Patsy was never the same after we returned to Monticello. From the start, I lived with the Mister, Patsy inside the big house and with my other family on Mulberry Row—my mother, James, my other brothers and sisters—men, women, and children spread out in the cabins on the mountaintop.

Four days after Christmas, I step out of the carriage.

(as young Sally) Oh, they're so surprised to see me in pretty clothes, skirt draped à la polonaise.

It's my first, so I don't show. *Elle n'a pas l'air.* Till Mother places her hand on my dress, through many layers of clothes. *Enciente.*

Patsy's still writing at the table. She hasn't looked my way, but she knows I'm here. She's probably going to tell me again there's no way to put it in writing, no way she can meet my demand.

(as Patsy) Haven't I suffered enough? Haven't I, Sally?

(as Sally) The Mistress of Monticello? You—a grand lady? You've suffered?—

Her face is as red as her father's the day he ordered her home from the convent.—

(as Sally) Patsy, I mean Mistress Randolph, were your children born into slavery? Did you see your own people sold away?

(as Patsy) Don't you sass me, you hear?

Patsy thinks she watches over the plantation. Although Patsy is the one who presides at formal occasions, I, Sally, who, strictly speaking, happen to be Patsy's aunt, actually run the place. Patsy likes this arrangement. She knows if another woman, a wife by the book, were to marry the Mister and move to this little mountain, she would have no authority. Better me than a competitor.

I try to speak sweetly.

(as Sally) Mistress Randolph, I do apologize.

(as Patsy) Your people? Did you ever harvest the wheat or feel the sun beating down on your face? Your people, the Hemings? They were never sold. Were they, Sally?

I struggle to keep my hands away from my ear. She's desperate now. She'll do anything to get me to leave all this alone. I want to ask her if she's ever harvested wheat, but she'll accuse me of sassing. There are things I've always wanted to say, but I'll hold off for now.

(to Patsy) My people? But I thought this was all our family… Didn't your father say that? That everyone in the cabins on Mulberry Row—at Monticello—we were all one family?

(as Patsy) Impudent…

I barely hear her say the word.

All across the county, all the families are large ones, spread out from the big house all across the farms. I was not the only slave with long flowing hair.

I know there's gossip on the neighboring farms. The tales have come back to me. You know some say the Mister grabs me—like this **(grabs her hair)**—and drags me into his bed. That he does that every night… All this hair? See how far it goes down my back? Just imagine how sore my head would be!

All the highborn gentlemen say they're against race-mixing. James says that's why the attendance is so high at the mulatto balls in Charlottesville. Of course black men are not allowed. The places are packed with white gentleman and young bright-yellow girls, so many there's barely room to breathe. I'm told there are numerous fights and scuffles outside the halls over the favors of these young girls. Only the physically strong dare go there.

Of course the Mister is against all such nonsense… dancing, even before marriage, is a highly questionable activity. Besides, he has sworn to be faithful to me as long as he lives.

I don't mean to give the impression that the Mister was the most somber of men. To the contrary. In the daytime, he never walked past me without singing **(hums to herself)**. **(Looks around, peeks through a doorway)** Everything's so quiet now. I can't bear the silence.

When he didn't care to be disturbed, they'd bring his meals to his room. Now there's a constant parade of important people, dignitaries, in and out!

(Looks towards his door.) Back then, no one dared to open his door—no one except me.

One after another our children are born. My mother Betty Hemings had an expression—she used to say all John Wayles had to do was put his shoes under her bed. That's all it took. It was that way with us too.

One October morning in 1795 our little girl is born, a babe who lives two years. 1798, a boy Beverley, 1799, another daughter, a sickly child.

When the Mister goes to Washington, I never seem to get help with the children. Patsy says there aren't enough hands to go around

Old shoe, our child is frail. This time pray with me. Pray she has strength. Glory be to God. Hosanna in the highest.

Did I tell you, Lord? Patsy's child had a fine funeral, gloves passed out by the hundreds, buried in the family plot. Not like my baby girl.

Old Shoe is in one of his moods:

(as young Sally) You want me to be more discreet. Not so obvious.

(as young Sally) I see, more careful.

(folds her arms as Jefferson would)

(as Jefferson) We must not draw attention to our situation.

(as young Sally) Our situation. Old Shoe. Of course not, I wouldn't dream of making a spectacle of myself. Of course, with a belly round as mine and this boy hanging on my leg,—Beverley—*Beverley*, I said hold on to the railing—why would I even think of it?

They say let a man have his ways. Make a little home. Don't question him when he goes away.

You want me to open the drawer? Mister, earbobs all the way from Philadelphia!

An odd pair of earrings, stately and solemn. He calls them a work of architecture—I mean art—if you can say that about earbobs. They remind me of the doorbell on the nail factory door. Large, heavy, my ear hangs down like so. **(She turns to face him.)** But when he puts them on me, very carefully, his fingers ever so gently touching my face, my heart is light. And I don't mind the way my earlobes droop. There's been no other woman in his bed. A promise kept.

Was I wrong? Should I have stayed in France? Who can calculate those things? The Mister might think he can, but only the Lord knows that answer. And what if I had changed my mind? Then what? I've lived the best I could. A new mattress when a babe's born, a girl to tend the children when the Mister's home. Extraordinary privileges, considering the way my people live on Mulberry Row.

The Mister does not want to be seen as a slaveholder. A difficult task indeed. With the right people, however, the Mister can relax and be the family man.

The day Dolly and James Madison came to sit with me in the small parlor—it was a pleasant occasion. A girl brought out the tea. The new babe was nestled beside me. The Mister was quiet at first then he began to go on and on about all the hard times he'd had the past few years trying to grow artichokes and figs until I thought I would get the worst headache. His concern for crop rotation… I had been in bed several weeks but was starting to mend. Dolly Madison took great pains to admire our little boy. Called him darling. Took her fingers and made curls with his mess of red hair. Wanted to hold him so badly. I motioned to the Mister. He nodded and smiled rather faintly. "Can I name him after my husband?" she asked. "Allow me the privilege, and you'll have the finest gift."

Oh, I'm not the sort of woman who holds a grudge. Definitely not, but Dolly Madison named my boy and promised me a fine gift, a hat with plumes. I never received one.

(calls out) James Madison, we called him Madison. Sit down over there. Right now. He's the busiest child. Madison and Eston are playing Storm the Bastille. The noise is deafening. Their father is largely responsible. He taught them to play the fiddle. All the boys—Eston, Beverley, Madison—but that wasn't enough.

(as Sally) Madison, leave your brother alone.

Thomas Jefferson loves war games, the rowdier and louder the better.

(to Eston) Eston, stand still. Bow for your father. Now raise your fiddle slowly. And one and two and…

(Crosses stage.)

Here comes Patsy, again… She's so tired and pale much of the time, and it doesn't help that she has to climb those stairs every night I know its hot up there in the summer and cold in the winter, and there's barely room to breathe. It's been twenty years and she's still talking about it.

(as Patsy) After those vermin finished dragging our name through the mud, it's a wonder we dare invite any guests to Monticello. You know how people are.

(as Sally) Oh, I thought we had a lovely evening, Mistress Randolph.

(as Patsy) Lovely? **(They laugh together.)** Wasn't Squire Denby's vest the most peculiar color? **(Beat)**

Do you think they've forgotten? This is what they've been waiting for... a chance to make a mockery of our good name. I was willing to ignore everything, Sally, all of it, but now

… We hold each other. At that moment, as close in age as we are, I am almost her mother.

(as Patsy) Now that he's going to leave us…you're asking too much. Sally, can't you see what this is doing to us?

In March, 1801, the Mister was victorious. He defeated Adams for the presidency, but the stories about him and me, they wouldn't stop. When I come in, the Mister folds his paper, hides away the news. He looks straight ahead, thinks he's being clever.

So many papers—so many stories about me and the Mister and the songs…

(starts to sing)

Of all the damsels on the green,

> On mountain, or in valley,

A lass so luscious ne'er was seen,

> As Monticellian Sally.

Yankee doodle, who's the noodle?

> What wife were half so handy?

To breed a flock of slaves for stock,

> A blackamoor's the dandy.

(Holds up newspapers.)

Papers—I've never seen so many.

"Marry a woman of your own complexion."

Quadroon, octoroon. "Whiter than white. Near white."

White? Near-white? Joined by common law.

On nights when dinner guests are served, I stand behind thick velvet drapes. Surprised when country squire can name the dish before him. The guests leave late.

After I finished putting away the Mister's linens, he asks me to sit beside him on the bed. He has a letter from Philadelphia. James has met difficulty after difficulty. So many chefs in the city. No call to hire a black man to do a white man's job. James drinks to hide the pain. The room was dark except for a small candle near his bed. I hear the words but I don't respond. The Mister repeats them again. James has hung himself. I don't hear those words. I hear James's footsteps. He's bringing up a plate of Charlotte Russe from the hotel kitchen. I hear him lecturing to me about the Mister, about freedom, but James is gone.

The Mister holds me down while we cry together for James. Old Shoe, I blame myself for begging my brother to return to America. Old Shoe, I blame you for insisting that he return. I chose to go back to the United States only to see my brother kill himself.

James, **(screams)** James, where are you now when I need you?

The candles are burning tonight. In every room in the house, the candles are burning, so different from the old days. Even when I was a girl, in the evening after dinner, we never saw so much light.

(as James) You're in the fish market now. Go ahead. Strike a bargain.

(Crosses stage)

Tonight I'll see the Mister.

Patsy is snuffing out the lights around the parlor.

(as Patsy) Sally, I thought you had left. Sally…

I try to ignore her, pretend I don't hear her calling me, but it's too late.

(to Patsy) You want me to wait till tomorrow? After he's had a good night's rest?

(to Patsy) He tired himself out entertaining the guests at dinner? Squire Denby and his stories about The Battle of Yorktown? I'm sorry, I can't wait.

She orders me away from his door, but I ignore her…

Before we left France he told me that Patsy must never be reminded of this. Never. But Patsy always knew, didn't she?

(Knocks at the door gently, then walks into the Mister's room.)

I stay here with the Mister in his suite of rooms on the first floor. His sanctum sanctorum. Everyone else must trudge up the stairs to their quarters, a narrow little passageway up to the top floor. It's always been that way. Why should it be any different tonight?

I stand beside his bed. I stood here four years ago the night our daughter Harriet left, walked away to live in white society. I spent weeks preparing the clothes for her trip— embroidering the hems of her skirts. Harriet was exceedingly beautiful, tall like her father, with copper red hair.

(to Harriet) Stand still, Harriet. Stand still while I fix your hem.

I can still hear her crying—all day and half the night.

(to Harriet) You ask me why you have to leave?

I told her about a woman on a neighboring farm, as white as the whitest ghost. She was known as the master's child. Never married, stayed in the house and grew like a plant without sun. Never walked away. They say she stayed in the house fifty years, knitting and weaving yarn, until one day she died.

The night she left Monticello for Washington, I took her in to see her father. The room was dark. I stood by the door. She knelt down and kissed his hands then began to cry again.

(as Jefferson) Harriet, get off your knees. It's time to go. Beverley's waiting for you.

(to Harriet) Harriet, stand up. Stand up! Do you hear your father? It's time to go.

When she left, I handed her a beaded bag of many colors— pink, purple, green, strung together, and in tiny gilt beads across the front, I had written *Harriet*. Inside... my gold cross, a watch from her father and 50 dollars.

Tonight I stand beside his bed again. Dark, winter, blue-black evening; la vie nocturne.

(to Jefferson) Mister, do you remember a Madame so-and-so who did not wear her jewelry well or arrange her hair?

(to Jefferson) Patsy tells me the will was completed yesterday. She says it's a good will.

(to Jefferson) You say you meant it to be? You say it was all you had to give to your family—all you could leave to them. I understand.

(to Jefferson) But it doesn't free Madison and Eston.

(to Jefferson) You say they'll be freed just as Beverly and Harriet were?

Is he serious? I pull at his flannel shirt. He's sitting on the side of the bed with his arms folded as if he's talking about how many covered dishes to have the cook set out the next evening or the number of guests staying the night. All so simple. Does he remember? Beverley and Harriet walked away from Monticello after months and months of the two of us planning for their safety.

(to Jefferson, incredulously) As Beverley and Harriet were freed?

Even sitting on the bed, he is a tall man. His hair is as white as his flannel shirt. He calls me Sally, love. Beverley and Harriet walked away, he tells me. We'll do the same for Madison and Eston.

"We"? What do you mean "we"? Who'll do this after you're gone? Who'll help me then? **(screams loudly)**

(as Sally moves closer to him.) Tom!

He sat erect, as if a bolt of lightning had just gone right through him. **(Raises her head to look straight at him.)**

(to Jefferson) Old Shoe? **(Takes his hand.)**

(to Jefferson) Old Shoe. We spent months, the two of us, making plans for Beverley to go to Washington. Then sending Harriet there to meet him. Who'll take care of all that if anything happens to you?

(laughs) You think I'm rushing you along? **(Sheepish laugh)**

Have I been happy with you? You have to ask that?

Maybe you think I'm being selfish, bringing all this up at a time like this, but I made my choice when we were in Paris together, and now I'm waiting to see. oh, I know some things, never work out the way you mean them to—but this time… this time…

(Throws herself on the bed, unravels hair)

(to Jefferson) Mister, it has to be legal. Real freedom. Not just walking off and running the risk of being sold away. On the run for the rest of their lives. Madison and Eston, I want them to be as free as any white child.

(to Jefferson) I know they look white… you know that's not enough. Look at Mulberry Row—slaves whiter than some white folks. Beverley at dusk—he could have been you.

(to Jefferson) You say nothing is stronger than our love?

(to Jefferson) Old shoe, I never doubted it.

Dark, winter, blue-black evening; la vie nocturne. Mister, I remember. Do you remember too? He said.

(as Jefferson) I'd do anything for you.

(as Sally) I remember. For days, you begged me to return. **(Sally remembering Jefferson's words)** "Come back to America. No work to stain your tender hands, the run of the house."

(as Jefferson) I swore to be faithful.

(as Sally) And you have been… you gave me your word. Thomas Jefferson, you haven't danced at a ball in forty years.

(as Jefferson) I never regretted it—never—but Patsy… She's been through so much and my grandchildren… to have it all revealed.

(as Sally) Revealed? What? You mean the shame of having a slave for a wife.

(as Jefferson) You are my wife.

(as Sally) Oh, I know I've never lived as a slave—not really—I know what they talk about. Not that we slept together. It wasn't that. That wasn't the shame. You brought me home—to live with you as your wife.

You gave your word—that you'd be faithful to me. I never doubted you not even once. Your word… you made a solemn promise to me, a slave: at twenty-one our children would be free.

(as Jefferson) My word is everything to me.

(as Sally) I know it is.

(as Jefferson) But the family—not just you and the boys—Patsy, her children, her grandchildren—all of you…

(as Sally) All of us—do this for all your children. Forget about me.

(as Jefferson) But you <u>are</u> my wife.

(as Sally) And I always will be, but I'm not asking to have my name in the will. I'll take my chances to see my children free.

(as Sally) Old shoe, after you've gone, I can leave. Quietly—walk away…

(Reaches up to him) No, No, don't. **(She puts her fingers to her lips.)** Don't—please. I know. I know that's not what you wanted… Old Shoe…

It's fine for me, —but our children—it will never be right for them. I can't take that chance. Freedom, they have to see for themselves, see it, see what it's like.

I hand him the pen. He begins to write the words that will free Madison and Eston.

Thomas Jefferson is known for being a stubborn man. He's used to having things exactly the way he wants them, and if they aren't… Of course, there are things I must understand. He insists a lady should not dance after she is married. I remember the dancing in Mulberry Row after the harvest, in the evening, so dizzy I fall to the ground, but I must agree to this. In turn, he swears he will never take the floor at cotillions. Singing, playing the fiddle, the harpsichord. All these are permissible. I giggle nervously. He glares at

40

me sternly. And I agree. I agree for as long as we both shall live.

THE END

Made in the USA
Coppell, TX
07 August 2020

32591733R00024